LEGO CITY ADVENTURES

HELP IS ON THE WAY!

By Sonia Sander

By Sonia Sander
Illustrated by Mada Design

SCHOLASTIC INC.

NEW YORK   TORONTO   LONDON   AUCKLAND

SYDNEY   MEXICO CITY   NEW DELHI   HONG KONG

ISBN-13: 978-0-545-15068-2 ISBN-10: 0-545-15068-X

LEGO, the LEGO logo, the Brick and the Knob configurations and the MiniFigure are trademarks of the LEGO Group. © 2009 The LEGO Group. All rights reserved.

Published by Scholastic Inc. SCHOLASTIC and associated logos are trademarks and/or registered trademarks of Scholastic Inc.

Used under license by Scholastic Inc. All rights reserved. Published by Scholastic Inc. SCHOLASTIC and associated logos are trademarks and/or registered trademarks of Scholastic Inc.

40 39 38 37 36 35 34 33 32 31   18 19/0

Printed in the U.S.A.   40
First printing, November 2009

Woof! Woof!
Jessie has a big dog named Bear.

Bear walks Jessie to school.
He barks at the cars as they cross.
Woof! Woof!
Beep! Beep!

Bear follows Jessie home, too. But today, Bear is not there. Uh-oh, where is Bear?

Jessie runs home but Bear is not there. "Bear! Bear!" she calls. "Come home, Bear!"

But he hasn't.
No one Jessie asks has seen Bear.
Oh, no, poor Bear is lost.

Drip! Drop! Drip! Drop!
It starts to rain.
"Where are you, Bear?"
Jessie cries.

Jessie hears Bear cry.
She finds him in the park.
Poor Bear is stuck under a gate!

Bear needs help fast.
Jessie asks the police for help.

Bear needs to be dug out.
The police call in even more help.

Splish! Splosh! Splat!
The rain gets worse.
It is too hard to dig in the mud.

C-r-r-r-e-e-a-a-k-k!
Jessie's new friends lift
the gate off Bear.

The workers take good care of Bear. They wrap up his paw.

Bear gives Jessie a big, wet kiss.
Jessie hugs Bear.
She says, "Now we can go home!"

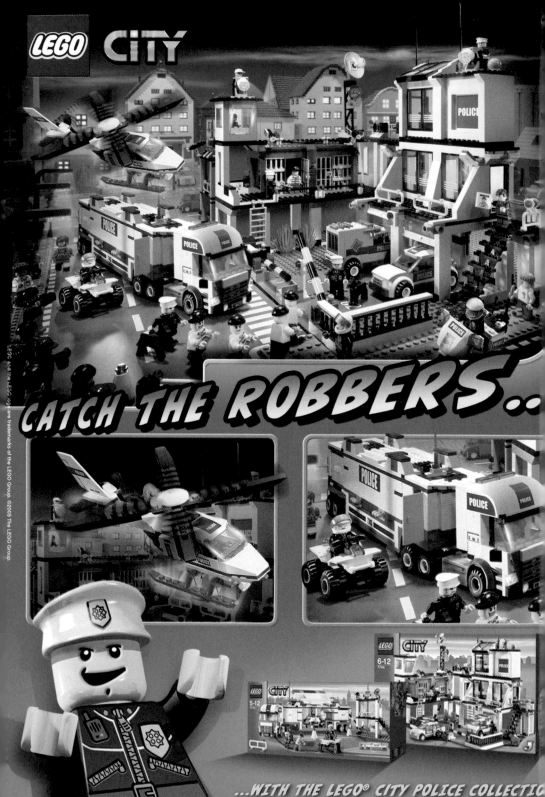

LEGO CITY

CATCH THE ROBBERS...

...WITH THE LEGO® CITY POLICE COLLECTIO

- Catch the robbers with the police truck
- Take them to the police station
- Lock them up in the prison block